March, 1996

P9-AQD-804

Bein' with You This Way

written by **W. Nikola-Lisa**
illustrated by **Michael Bryant**

Scholastic Inc.

New York Toronto London Auckland Sydney

No part of this publication may be reproduced in whole or in part, or stored in
a retrieval system, or transmitted in any form, or by any means, electronic,
mechanical, photocopying, recording, or otherwise, without written permission
of the publisher. For information regarding permission, write to
Lee & Low Books, Inc., 95 Madison Avenue, New York, NY 10016.

ISBN 0-590-80804-4

Text copyright © 1994 by W. Nikola-Lisa.
Illustrations copyright © 1994 by Michael Bryant.
All rights reserved. Published by Scholastic Inc., 555 Broadway,
New York, NY 10012, by arrangement with Lee & Low Books, Inc.

12 11 10 9 8 7 6 5 4 3 2 1   6 7 8 9/9 0 1/0

Printed in Hong Kong

First Scholastic printing, January 1996

To the beauty of people,
the wonder of childhood—W.N.L.

For my wife, Gina,
and my children, Kristen and Allison,
whose laughter and giggles help me
remember the joy of childhood—M.B.

Hey, everybody, are you ready?
 Uh-huh!
Then snap those fingers
and tap those toes,
and sing along with me.

All right!
Here we go...

She has straight hair.
He has curly hair.
How perfectly
remarkably
strange,
Uh-huh!

Straight hair.
Curly hair.
Different—
Mm-mmm,
but the same,
Ah-ha!

Now isn't it beautiful,
 simply unusual,
bein' with you
 this way!

Say, what a big nose!
Hey, what a little nose!
How perfectly
 remarkably
 strange,
 Uh-huh!

Big nose.
  Little nose.
Straight hair.
  Curly hair.
Different—
  Mm-mmm,
but the same,
  Ah-ha!

Now isn't it satisfying,
  simply electrifying,
bein' with you
  this way!

Now his eyes are brown.
And her eyes are blue.
How perfectly
    remarkably
       strange,
Uh-huh!

Brown eyes.
   Blue eyes.
Big nose.
   Little nose.
Straight hair.
   Curly hair.
Different—
   Mm-mmm,
but the same,
   Ah-ha!

I said isn't it incredible,
  simply unforgettable,
bein' with you
  this way!

Wow, those are thick arms!
Hey, those are thin arms!
  How perfectly
    remarkably
      strange,
Uh-huh!

Thick arms.
  Thin arms.
Brown eyes.
  Blue eyes.
Big nose.
  Little nose.
Straight hair.
  Curly hair.
Different—
  Mm-mmm,
but the same,
  Ah-ha!

Now isn't it fabulous,
  simply enrapturous,
bein' with you
  this way!

Look at those long legs!
Look at those short legs!
 How perfectly
  remarkably
   strange,
 Uh-huh!

Long legs.
 Short legs.
Thick arms.
 Thin arms.
Brown eyes.
 Blue eyes.
Big nose.
 Little nose.
Straight hair.
 Curly hair.
Different—
 Mm-mmm,
but the same,
 Ah-ha!

Now isn't it terrific,
simply exquisite,
bein' with you
this way!

Her skin is light.
His skin is dark.
How perfectly
remarkably
strange,
Uh-huh!

Light skin.
　Dark skin.
Long legs.
　Short legs.
Thick arms.
　Thin arms.
Brown eyes.
　Blue eyes.
Big nose.
　Little nose.
Straight hair.
　Curly hair.
Different—
　Mm-mmm,
but the same,
　Ah-ha!

Now isn't it delightful,
　simply out-of-sightful,
bein' with you
　this way!

I said, isn't it delightful,
totally insightful,
bein' with you
this way!

Be-bop-a-doo-bop.
 Be-bop-boo.
Be-bop-a-doo-bop.
 Doo-be-dee-doo.

Oh yeah!

Be-bop-a-doo-bop.
Be-bop-boo.
Be-bop-a-doo-bop.
Doo-be-dee-doo.

Mm-mmm!

Be-bop-a-doo-bop.
Be-bop-boo.
Be-bop-a-doo-bop.
Doo-be-dee-doo.

That's right!

And we're gonna be like this
all the rest of our lives,
so come and be with us...

we're on our way!

HEY!